Help!

SALLY GRINDLEY and PETER UTTON

There's a Big Bad Wolf inside this book and we need to catch him!

𝘩
Hodder
Children's
Books

He's a pest!

He's really scary!

The Big Bad Wolf looks like this. Will you help us catch him? You'll have to be quiet, because he mustn't know we're here.

Peep through that window in case he's inside.
What can you see?
All right, let's get going now, because
we need to catch that wolf.

What things shall we take to catch him?
A ladder? Some boots?
You choose.

Be very quiet and keep a lookout
for the Big Bad Wolf.
We must catch him, before he catches us.

Check in the trees and under the bridge and in the hen house. Is he there? Now peek through the fence, in case he's waiting to pounce. OK, let's turn the page.

Oh no! That was no sheep. It was the Big Bad Wolf,
and look what he's done to that house!

We must catch him before he does any more harm.
Turn the page quickly and let's go after him.

Which way did he go?
Make sure he's not hiding anywhere.

We need to hurry. Turn over the page and let's see if he's there.

He went this way,

or was it that way?

He must have gone through the hedge.
Have a look and see if he's there.

We must keep going.
There's no time to lose if
we're going to catch that wolf.

Mooo!

It's only a
spotty cow.

We need to hurry.
Turn over the page
and see if he's there.

Do you think that cat is the wolf? I don't think so, but the wolf might be in there somewhere. Let's creep in and have a look. Turn over the page very quietly.

Open that cupboard door
and see if the wolf is in there.

Do you think he's under the bed?
Be very quiet and have a look.

Help! Turn the page before he catches us!

Well done, everyone!
Now, what shall we do with him?

Let's turn the page and help him leave the book.

one, two, three...

Quick! Shut the book so he can't get back in!

For the one and only Gus Franks
S.G.

For Anke
P.U.

HODDER CHILDREN'S BOOKS

First published in Great Britain in 2015 by Hodder and Stoughton
This paperback edition published 2016.

A CIP catalogue record of this book
is available from the British Library.

ISBN: 978 1 444 92474 9

10 9 8 7 6 5 4 3 2 1

Printed and bound in China

Hodder Children's Books
An imprint of Hachette Children's Group
Part of Hodder and Stoughton
Carmelite House
50 Victoria Embankment
London EC4Y 0DZ

An Hachette UK Company
www.hachette.co.uk

www.hachettechildrens.co.uk